# Play Day
# School Day

For kids who love to play and learn
And for kids who love to learn and play
Every day

First edition 2020. Library of Congress Catalog Card Number pending. ISBN 978-1-5362-0283-0. This book was typeset in Avenir. The illustrations were created with ink, pencil, pastel, cut paper, torn tissue paper, and digital collage. Candlewick Press, 99 Dover Street, Somerville, Massachusetts 02144. visit us at www.candlewick.com Printed in Dongguan, Guangdong, China. 20 21 22 23 24 25 TLF 10 9 8 7 6 5 4 3 2 1

# Play Day
# School Day

CANDLEWICK PRESS

**"Tomorrow is the first day of school,"
says Mona. "I can't wait to go back!"**

"What do you do at school?" asks Milo.
"Lots of things," says Mona.

"Like what?" Milo asks.

"Like ride a school bus . . .

## "Practice reading and writing . . .

"Learn about science . . .

"math,

"art, and music.

**"Sometimes at school, you sit still and listen carefully . . .**

"And sometimes you run and run and get to be loud with your friends."

"School sounds fun!"
says Milo.

"It is," says Mona.
"And so is playing with you."